Class act

Joshua had never seen a goon. The boys in third grade weren't permitted to draw pictures on the blackboard.

"We make goon pictures on the blackboard of whoever drives us crazy," Brendan said. "You do one, Joshua."

Joshua took the chalk and examined the goons with their swollen heads. He had in mind Mr. Regan. First Joshua drew an enormous head. Then he drew a small square body and long sticks for legs going straight down to the bottom of the blackboard. He was concentrating on dotting the face with freckles when Ethan whispered, "Here comes Mr. Regan," and Douglas said, "Quick, Josh, find a seat," and in a second the crowd around the blackboard had dispersed, had taken seats in the classroom and opened their books as if they had been studying all along.

So Joshua T. Bates was left at the blackboard drawing Mr. Regan as a goon.

"Joshua Bates," Mr. Regan said. "Welcome to the fourth grade."

Joshua T. Bates
in Trouble Again

Susan Shreve

illustrated by
Roberta Smith

A KNOPF PAPERBACK
Alfred A. Knopf · New York

for Nicholas

A KNOPF PAPERBACK PUBLISHED BY ALFRED A. KNOPF

Text copyright © 1997 by Susan Shreve
Illustrations copyright © 1997 by Roberta Smith
Cover art copyright © 1997 by John Ward

Visit us on the Web! www.randomhouse.com/kids

Educators and librarians, for a variety of teaching tools, visit us at **www.randomhouse.com/teachers.**

Library of Congress Cataloging-in-Publication Data
Shreve, Susan Richards.
Joshua T. Bates in trouble again/ by Susan Shreve.
p. cm.
Summary: After finally being promoted to fourth grade in the middle of the year, Joshua is so worried about the bully who rules the fourth-grade boys that he makes some unwise decisions.
[1. Schools—Fiction. 2. Bullies—Fiction. 3. Family life—Fiction.
4. Self-reliance—Fiction.]
I. Smith, Roberta, 1949- ill. II. Title.
PZ7.S55915Jn 1997
[Fic]—dc21 97-15589
ISBN: 0-375-80675-x (promotional edition)
       0-679-88520-x (trade)
       0-679-985240-4 (lib. bdg.)
       0-679-89263-x (pbk.)

First Knopf Paperback edition: September 1998

Printed in the United States of America

May 2000

10 9 8 7 6 5 4 3 2 1

OPM

Joshua T. Bates
in Trouble Again

Chapter One

It was still dark when Joshua Bates woke up on the Monday morning after Thanksgiving for his first day in the fourth grade at Mirch Elementary. And it was gloomy with a strong wind banging against the windows.

He had been looking forward to this day for a very long time. But on this stormy morning, his knees weak, his brain a jumble of worries, he wished today was over and he was waking up to his second day of fourth grade.

He got out of bed, lifted Plutarch, his cross-eyed yellow cat, from the comforter where he was sleeping, turned on the light, and looked at himself in the long mirror on his closet door. He was not pleased.

He looked wrong, he decided. Completely wrong for fourth grade. Especially his hair. His flyaway hair, which had been fine in third grade, wouldn't work for fourth grade.

In the bathroom between his room and that of his

formerly smart sister Amanda, he got some mousse so his square-cut flyaway hair would stand up straight like the hair of his archenemy, Tommy Wilhelm.

It was important to look right. Especially because everyone else had already been in the fourth grade since September while Joshua had been stuck in third grade for the second year in a row.

His clothes were on his desk where his mother had laid them out—the usual brown corduroys and a long-sleeved red shirt and white socks. He stuffed them back into his bureau, choosing instead a pair of black jeans with a hole in the knee, an old blue-striped shirt of his father's that hung past his thighs, and a black sweatshirt with MIRCH ELEMENTARY on the back, which he tied around his waist.

Just as the light of dawn was crawling over the horizon, filling the upstairs of the Bates house on Lowell Street in Washington, D.C., with a silver-gray light, Joshua went into Amanda's room, walking stiffly so his hair wouldn't flop.

"What do you think?" he asked, standing beside her bed.

Before this fall, when Amanda started seventh grade at the junior high school, she had been the very best student at Mirch Elementary, best all-round student in sixth grade and top of the honor roll. But

something began to happen to her when she moved to Alice Deal Junior High. A few weeks after school started, she cut her hair in long bangs that covered her eyes, painted her toenails black, and, according to her first report card, she was no longer smart.

She opened her eyes.

"What do I think about what?" she asked.

He shrugged.

"About how I look," he said.

Amanda sat up and drew her knees under her chin.

"You've put Vaseline or maple syrup in your hair." She reached over and touched his hair. "Is that what you mean?"

"It's mousse."

"My mousse?" Amanda asked.

"I don't have any mousse myself," Joshua said. "I *had* to use it. Every guy in the fourth grade wears it."

Amanda climbed out of bed and threw open the door to her closet.

"I think it's a bad look for you, Joshua," she said, pulling a tiny black skirt off the hanger. "You should look the same as you always look." She smiled sweetly. "Sort of nerdy."

Nerdy was exactly Joshua's fear. The name Tommy Wilhelm had called him on the soccer field during his second year in the third grade.

"I don't want to look nerdy," Joshua said, feeling the top of his moussed hair. "That's the point."

"I don't know about the shirt, Joshua," his mother said, coming out of her bedroom carrying one-year-old Georgianna, who had squashed banana all over her plump face. "It looks sloppy."

"That's how it's supposed to look," Joshua said. "Sloppy is a fourth-grade look."

His mother kissed the top of his head.

"Andrew doesn't seem to look sloppy," she said.

"Andrew doesn't care what he wears," he said of his best friend forever since kindergarten. "But boys like Tommy Wilhelm wear their fathers' shirts," he said. "I checked into it."

"I wouldn't worry about how you look, sweetheart," his mother said, carrying Georgianna downstairs. "I've always admired your independent mind, which is more than I can say about the mind of Tommy Wilhelm."

But Joshua was worried. He was worried about everything, and he had reason.

On Labor Day, Joshua had found out from his parents that he had flunked third grade.

"That's not possible," he said. "I've already been in third grade once and I won't go twice."

"Of course you have, darling," his mother replied, "but the teachers feel that you need another year to mature."

"Well, they're wrong," he said. "What do they expect at nine years old? I'm very mature already. I'm more mature than Tommy Wilhelm."

But not one of the teachers at Mirch Elementary agreed with Joshua. And so during the month of September of his second year in third grade, Joshua Bates almost died of humiliation. He was ridiculed by Tommy Wilhelm and the fourth-grade boys, teased by his sister Amanda, and left out of games.

But very soon after the beginning of the school year and thanks to Mrs. Goodwin, his new third-grade teacher, he made up his mind to be promoted.

Every day after school, he had worked with Mrs. Goodwin at her house or in the library or at her desk after school was out, getting better and better at reading and math. Just before Thanksgiving vacation, one month after his tenth birthday, he took a test for fourth grade and to everyone's surprise—especially Joshua's—he passed it.

"With flying colors," his mother said.

"A star performance," his father said.

And on Wednesday, the day before Thanksgiving, Mrs. Goodwin called him up to her desk to tell him that when he came back to school on Monday, he would be in Mr. Regan's fourth grade.

"I can't believe it," he had said to his mother that afternoon, helping her stuff the turkey for Thanksgiving dinner.

"You *should* believe it," she said to him. "You deserve it."

"You worked like a trouper," his father said.

That night, he was too excited to sleep.

On Friday, he had a sleepover with Andrew, and on Saturday he called his old friends—Brendan and Rusty and Ethan.

"Guess what?" he said to each of them. "I have good news. I'm going to be in fourth grade on Monday."

"Great," they said.

"I did amazing on the test."

"Great," they said again.

But they didn't make it sound great. They certainly didn't seem as excited as Joshua was. Not excited enough.

By Sunday, Joshua was upset.

"Maybe my old friends from last year won't be very glad to see me," he said to his mother after breakfast.

"Of course they will," his mother said.

"They didn't seem glad when I told them on the telephone yesterday," he said, sinking into a deep gloom.

"It will be different for them, Joshua," his mother said, sitting down in a chair next to him. "Change is hard, and they got used to your repeating third grade."

"Maybe I won't have any friends at all," Joshua said.

"You have friends already, darling," his mother said. "In a flash things will be back to normal, just like it was when all of you were in the third grade together."

"Maybe," Joshua said.

But he was sick with worry.

Once more before he left for school, Joshua checked himself in the mirror. Not bad, he thought, pleased with the long shirt flapping around his knees, especially pleased to see his hair could stand up like a small chair on his forehead.

He packed his book bag, kicked his dirty clothes under the bed, and waited until he heard his father going downstairs for breakfast. Then Joshua stopped by the bathroom, where Amanda was making faces at herself in the mirror.

"What are you doing?" he asked.

"Checking how I look," she said, smiling at herself

so her dimples were deep tunnels in her cheeks. "You know, checking my expressions so I'll know what other people see when they look at me."

"Weird," Joshua said, leaning against the door.

"I never thought about how I looked until this year. I just *was*." She turned off the bathroom light and went into her bedroom to finish dressing. "It's not easy being young."

"I know," Joshua said. "Things change too fast."

He went downstairs and slipped into a chair next to Georgianna, avoiding his father's eyes.

"Is that the way you're going to school, Joshua?" his father asked.

"It's the way fourth-grade boys dress," Joshua said. "All of them."

"Not *this* fourth-grade boy," his father began.

"Even Andrew dresses like this. Or almost," Joshua said. "You should call his mother."

But luckily for Joshua, Amanda sailed into the kitchen in black lipstick and dangly earrings and silver nail polish and sat down across the table from Joshua.

"Are you dressed for a costume party?" Mr. Bates asked.

Amanda looked up from her cereal. "Are you talking to me?"

"You can go upstairs and take the silver stuff off

your nails. It looks absurd. And that black lipstick, too."

"Plum," Amanda said. "Plum Passion, it's called. Mom wears it, too, sometimes."

"And the earrings," Mr. Bates said. "Now."

Amanda started to get up.

"You can dress up for parties, Amanda," Mrs. Bates said, always the more tolerant of Joshua's parents.

"I'm not dressed up," Amanda said. "This is the way the girls at Alice Deal Junior High School dress every day of their lives. And usually their skirts are up to their underpants." She stood up to leave. "So you're lucky I don't dress like that."

"We're very grateful, Amanda," Mr. Bates said as Amanda headed upstairs to wipe off her lipstick and take off the nail polish and earrings.

By the time she had gone upstairs, Mr. Bates had forgotten about Joshua.

In fact, his parents almost forgot that it was Joshua's first day of fourth grade until the telephone rang. It was Andrew calling to tell Joshua that he was sick.

"So I can't walk to school with you," Andrew said.

"Bummer," Joshua said sadly, a sudden hole in his stomach at the thought of walking to school alone, of spending the day without Andrew's friendship as protection.

"But call me when you get home to tell me how fourth grade is," Andrew said, his voice hoarse and weak.

"Sure," Joshua said, hanging up the phone. "Andrew's sick," he said crossly to his parents, as if he held them accountable. "So I have to go to school alone."

"I'm sorry about Andrew, darling," Mrs. Bates said. "But maybe it will be better to have no one but yourself to depend on today."

"I don't think so," Joshua said. "It will probably be worse."

And he opened the back door to leave.

"Good luck, pal," his father said, and his mother gave him a sloppy kiss that almost ruined his hair.

"It's too bad Dad made you change your outfit," Joshua said to Amanda when she flew up Lowell Street to catch up with him.

"No problem," she said. "I have the lipstick and earrings and nail polish in my book bag. I'll put them on as soon as I get to school."

"And then what?"

"I change back to the usual me before I come home from school."

"That's pretty weird," Joshua said.

Amanda shrugged. "Seventh grade is a little

weird," she agreed. "People smoke, you know. Especially the girls."

They came to the bus stop on Wisconsin Avenue, where the L4 stopped at 7:48 A.M.

"Have you ever tried smoking?" Amanda asked.

Joshua shook his head. "Never," he said. "Have you?"

"Never," Amanda said. "But your dumb friend Tommy Wilhelm does. I saw him outside the drugstore Friday night with Billy Nickel, leaning against the building, smoking."

"Smoking in fourth grade?" Joshua asked, amazed. "I can't believe it."

"It's probably illegal. They should be arrested," Amanda said, getting on the bus that would take her to Alice Deal Junior High. "I hope fourth grade is better than third," she called.

"Me too," Joshua said, and he hurried down Wisconsin Avenue, a little late, thinking of Tommy Wilhelm smoking outside the drugstore.

Joshua watched the bus with his sister in it move up Wisconsin Avenue, and then he walked past Newark and Ordway and Porter Street, pausing occasionally by a storefront window to check his reflection in the shadowed glass.

Then, just before he crossed Nebraska Avenue two

blocks below Mirch Elementary, his eye caught a bright white cigarette lying on the grass beside the curb. It was a clean cigarette, a little squashed but unsmoked, and instinctively he picked it up and put it behind his ear.

He and Amanda had seen an old movie a few weeks ago, and in it the hero kept a cigarette behind his ear. Joshua didn't see people smoking very often, except his grandfather smoking a pipe, and so it was memorable to see the actor in the movie with his cigarette. It made him look like Somebody.

And that's how Joshua felt, walking alone to his first day of fourth grade, worried—a lot worried—but very glad he'd found the cigarette just in case he met Tommy Wilhelm on the way to school.

Chapter Two

Tommy Wilhelm had been Joshua's enemy in first grade when he poured tomato juice in Joshua's milk thermos, and in second grade when he put worms in the pocket of Joshua's gym shorts, but especially lately, since Joshua flunked third grade.

"Tommy likes it when other boys have troubles," Joshua's mother told him in September when he started third grade for the second time.

"He's a creep," Joshua said crossly.

"Don't worry about him," his mother had said. "He's a bully and bullies have no courage. He will only attack a person he thinks is weak so he can win."

"I wish he'd explode and spontaneously combust and shatter in a million pieces and disappear," Joshua said to his mother. "But he won't."

The boys in the fourth grade were afraid of Tommy Wilhelm. They paid attention to what he told them and they liked the people he liked and didn't like the people he didn't like, which happened lately to include Joshua T. Bates.

It was cold with a strong wind blowing west and Joshua walked with his shoulders hunched against the chill, his head down so his moussed hair would stick up. When he saw Tommy Wilhelm coming up Thirty-fourth Street with his sidekick Billy Nickel trotting alongside him, he straightened and checked the cigarette behind his ear.

Tommy Wilhelm was taller than Joshua. He had a long birdlike face and short blond hair and bangs glued to stand up board-straight like a chair on his forehead. His backpack was slung over one shoulder, and he wore his brother's green and white high school basketball jacket that said WILSON H.S. #45 on the back. He walked a little like a bear, with one shoulder down, slouching, his feet shuffling along the sidewalk.

Other boys in the fourth grade copied the way Tommy walked, the way he dressed in his father's shirts and rumpled jeans, the way he talked out of the side of his mouth as if the other side were full of chewing gum.

"What's up?" Tommy asked.

"Not much," Joshua said, his heart beating a little too hard in his chest, his breath thin.

"So you finally go to fourth grade today," Tommy said. "Did you hear that, Billy?"

"Yeah," Billy Nickel said. "I heard."

"Right," Joshua said. "I did really well on the test."

He wished he hadn't added that. He wished he hadn't said anything that might give Tommy Wilhelm an advantage, a chance to make fun of him on his first day of fourth grade, three months late.

"You mean you've learned to read," Tommy said. "Very good news."

"Thanks a lot," Joshua said.

"Maybe you can read to us." Billy giggled, nudging Tommy in the ribs.

"Right," Joshua said. Right. It was all he could think to say. Right, right, right, when what he felt was wrong, wrong, wrong.

He wanted to take his cigarette out from behind his ear so they would notice that he had one. He could tap it on his finger, the way he'd seen it done in the movie he watched with Amanda. He wouldn't light it, of course, but he could put it between his thumb and forefinger as if he were going to light it, as if he knew what he was doing. He reached up and twisted the cigarette with his finger.

"Where'd you get that?" Tommy asked.

Joshua shrugged.

"Do you smoke?"

He didn't say yes because it wasn't the truth and he

was afraid to lie, especially about smoking cigarettes. But he wasn't going to say no, of course, since the whole reason for picking up the cigarette and putting it behind his ear in the first place was to protect himself from trouble, to seem what Amanda would call "groovy."

"We do," Billy said. "Me and Tommy."

"I heard," Joshua said.

"From who?" Tommy asked.

"From no one you know," Joshua said.

He wasn't going to tell on his sister, even though he sometimes wanted to string Amanda upside down in front of her full-length mirror so she could look at herself upturned, in her short, short skirt, her underwear showing. He didn't want to get her in trouble with Tommy Wilhelm. One member of the Bates family in trouble with Tommy was sufficient.

"Your sister," Tommy said. "I saw her yesterday at the drugstore."

"Yeah," Billy Nickel said. "Me too."

"We were together, dumbbell," Tommy said, bopping Billy Nickel on the head.

They started up the steps of Mirch Elementary, Joshua walking just ahead, pulling open the red door of the side entrance where the library was located.

Joshua had just reached up to remove the cigarette

and slip it into his jacket pocket since certainly he didn't want trouble on the first day of fourth grade, when Tommy stopped him.

"Don't," he said. "Leave it behind your ear. It's very cool."

And Joshua believed that he meant it. He felt his face flush, felt the pleasure rush through him in spite of himself, in spite of his distrust of Tommy Wilhelm.

"Yeah, cool," Billy Nickel said.

"It would take a lot of nerve to walk into the fourth grade on your first day after flunking and have a cigarette behind your ear," Tommy Wilhelm said.

"Right," Billy Nickel said.

Joshua thought about it for half a second, his heart racing, his common sense slipping away.

"Sure," he said, walking down the corridor past the library, the all-purpose room, the walls of fourth-grade projects on South Africa. "I'll do that. No problem."

Chapter Three

Joshua Bates had never been a "good" boy, as in obedient or orderly or "goody-goody," as his mother would say. But he hadn't been bad, either. He had never been in the kind of trouble that got him sent to the principal's office or kept him after school or got him suspended, as had happened to some of the boys he knew, including Billy Nickel. The only trouble he'd had was flunking third grade, and that he had not done on purpose.

He thought of himself as normal.

"Joshua's regular," Andrew said.

He was a good athlete, easygoing, dependable, and smart, in spite of the difficulty he had with reading; smart like an animal with a good sniffer.

"I'm just regular, like Andrew says," Joshua told his mother one afternoon earlier in the fall while he was repeating third grade, when she was complimenting him on his strength of character.

He wasn't interested in strength of character. He didn't, in fact, have any idea what character meant, but he loved his mother and he wasn't going to disappoint her and so he sat at the kitchen table and listened to her praise, thinking about soccer and whether he'd be able to play with the fourth graders.

"You're not a follower, Joshua," his mother said, making Georgianna's dinner. "Some boys you know are followers, trying to please whoever seems to be in charge, like Tommy Wilhelm." She ran her fingers through his hair. "You're not like that."

Joshua had shrugged.

Maybe he wasn't a follower and maybe he was. He didn't know anything anymore for sure. Like why having a cigarette made him feel cool, when he usually thought they were gross. Just when he thought he knew exactly the way he felt, things changed—like flunking third grade.

When Joshua Bates walked down the corridor past the library and the principal's office and the all-purpose room, Tommy Wilhelm was just ahead of him. Ethan and Rusty were waiting next to his locker.

"Catch a look at Joshua," Tommy said, passing Ethan, Billy Nickel close on his heels.

Joshua heard him, his heart beating so hard he was afraid it might leap out of his chest.

"Cigarette," Tommy whispered.

Ethan put his hands in his pockets, giving Joshua a funny look. "So've you got a new locker with the fourth graders yet?" he asked.

"Not yet," Joshua said, conscious of the cigarette behind his ear, certain that Ethan and Rusty had seen it and were intrigued.

"I'll get one today, I guess," he said. "I've got to get fourth-grade books."

"We're doing fractions," Ethan said in a "so there" kind of voice.

"I've done fractions," Joshua said.

"In third grade?" Rusty asked. "We didn't do fractions in third grade."

"Right," Joshua said. "I remember." He opened his old locker located just next to the fourth-grade lockers and hung up his jacket. "This third grade was pretty advanced because of Mrs. Goodwin," he said, walking with Rusty and Ethan past the third-grade classroom where he had gone every school day for the past three months, and waving at Mrs. Goodwin.

Just to see her, standing at the blackboard writing the date and the weather and the homework assignments, filled his heart with joy.

He had never particularly liked teachers until he had Mrs. Goodwin. Teachers had seemed to be a necessary

and unpleasant part of going to school, bad-tempered
about his reading, disappointed in his writing, irritated
with his math homework, generally unhappy with
Joshua.

But Mrs. Goodwin was different.

"I hear she's a battleship," Rusty said.

"Wrong. She's great," Joshua said. "The best
teacher I've ever had."

No one mentioned the cigarette behind his ear until he
got to the door of the fourth-grade classroom, and then
Ethan turned to him, cocked his head, and folded his
arms across his chest.

"Are you going to walk into class like that?" he
asked.

Joshua took a deep breath, his face prickly, his
stomach churning as if he had the flu. He was going to
walk into class with the cigarette behind his ear because it was too late to change his mind, but at that moment he would have been just as glad to put on his
jacket and hat and run all the way home.

"Why not?" Joshua asked, reaching up to check the
cigarette.

Ethan looked at Tommy Wilhelm, who was smiling
a broad, devilish smile.

He was impressed, Joshua could tell.

Douglas Baer was standing with Brendan beside the chalkboard making pictures, big-headed creatures with little tufts of hair on the tops of their heads and tiny spindly legs and arms going in all directions. He was very glad to see Joshua.

"Joshua Bates!" he said, throwing himself against Joshua, shoulder to shoulder, grabbing his head in a bear hug and laughing. "Did you know Joshua was coming to fourth grade today, Bren?" he asked Brendan.

Brendan was finishing the wobbly legs on his picture. "I knew Joshua was going to be here today because he called me on Saturday. "

"We're making goons," Douglas said to Joshua.

"Goons?" Joshua asked.

"We always make them," Brendan said. "It's a fourth-grade thing."

Joshua had never seen a goon. The boys in third grade weren't permitted to draw pictures on the blackboard, and he'd never heard of goons. The most he knew about fourth grade was holey jeans and long shirts and hair mousse. Goons were something new.

"We make goon pictures on the blackboard of whoever drives us crazy," Brendan said. "And then just before the bell when Mr. Regan comes from the teachers' room to the classroom, we fly to our seats, leave the goons on the blackboard, and open our math books like we've been studying math all morning."

Joshua folded his arms across his chest and examined the pictures.

"Can you tell who these are?" Douglas asked, pointing to the two goons he and Brendan had drawn on the blackboard.

"Do I know them?" Joshua asked.

"You know them," Brendan said. "One of them you know extremely well."

Tommy Wilhelm had joined them, and Rusty and Ethan were standing just behind.

"I don't," Joshua said. "Are they teachers?"

"Right." Brendan laughed.

"That's the principal," Tommy Wilhelm said. "Isn't that Mr. Barnes?"

"Exactly," Brendan said, pointing to the goon with a long mustache and very large teeth.

"And this guy without any hair is the phys. ed. guy," Douglas said.

"You do one, Joshua," Brendan said.

"Like who?" Joshua asked.

"Like you do it and we guess," Douglas said.

"It can be a teacher or anyone?" Joshua asked.

"That's right," Ethan said.

Joshua took the chalk and examined the goons with

their swollen heads. He had in mind Mr. Regan. Mr. Regan was young, with thin blond hair that he wore in bangs. He had a tiny body, much too small for his long, long legs, and he had freckles like mad all over his face and nose and ears and neck.

First Joshua drew an enormous head. Then he drew a small square body and long sticks for legs going straight down to the bottom of the blackboard. He was concentrating on dotting the face with freckles when Ethan whispered, "Here comes Mr. Regan," and Douglas said, "Quick, Josh, find a seat," and in a second the crowd around the blackboard had dispersed, had taken seats in the classroom and opened their books as if they had been studying all along.

So Joshua T. Bates was left at the blackboard drawing Mr. Regan as a goon.

"Joshua Bates," Mr. Regan said. "Welcome to the fourth grade."

He stuck out his hand and shook Joshua's.

"For today," Mr. Regan said to Joshua, "you can sit in the back of the room between Tommy Wilhelm and Rusty."

He opened his roll book.

"Okay?" Mr. Regan asked.

"Okay," Joshua said.

Nervously Joshua slid into the empty seat between

Rusty and Tommy, conscious of people's eyes on him, on his fourth-grade outfit, on his stand-up hair, on the cigarette stuck behind his ear, just white enough and small enough to almost disappear. He knew, though, that his classmates could see it.

"So you know about goons, Joshua," Mr. Regan was saying.

"I just found out today," Joshua said quietly.

"This goon looks very familiar," Mr. Regan said, erasing the Mr. Barnes goon and the phys. ed. goon.

The fourth grade giggled and buried their heads in their arms.

"Is this your artwork, Joshua?" Mr. Regan asked.

Joshua hesitated.

"I don't need to ask you, of course, since you were drawing this goon when I came into the classroom." He folded his arms, examining the picture. "Now, who at Mirch Elementary could you have had in mind with all those freckles?"

Joshua held his breath.

Mr. Regan wasn't smiling. He didn't seem to be particularly angry, but he didn't seem pleased or funny or lighthearted exactly, or any of the things Joshua might have hoped for from his new teacher.

He erased Joshua's picture from the legs up to the enormous freckled head. "Good-bye, Mr. Regan," he said, checking the clock over the door. "Nine o'clock."

First he called roll—only Andrew was absent—and then he made announcements and handed out a notice for food collections during the December holidays, and finally he said, "Take out your math books and turn to page 107."

He looked over at Joshua.

"Do you have a fourth-grade math book?" he asked.

"I don't," Joshua said.

Mr. Regan took a math book from the bookcase behind his desk. "Here you are."

Joshua got up and walked to the front of the room.

"And Joshua," Mr. Regan said coolly. "Would you please give me the cigarette you seem to be keeping behind your ear?"

Joshua took the cigarette and handed it to Mr. Regan. Behind him, he could feel the eyes of the fourth graders burning into his back, especially Tommy Wilhelm's. But when he turned around, everyone was pretending to read, except Tommy, who watched Joshua walk back up the row of desks and take his seat.

Chapter Four

Joshua's first day in fourth grade was not going well.

First there was the problem with the goons and then the cigarette and then he flunked a math quiz first period and everyone in the class knew about it.

To Joshua's horror, the quizzes were corrected in class. Everyone traded papers with the person sitting on his or her right and Mr. Regan read the answers. Rusty traded papers with Joshua. Rusty got a 90 and Joshua got a 30.

"Never mind, Joshua," Mr. Regan said after the scores had been read out. "This material is new to you."

But he did mind, of course. It didn't matter whether the material was new to him or not, now everyone in the class knew he got a 30 on a math quiz, which was not a good way to begin fourth grade when he already had a reputation for flunking third.

At least when the bell rang for the next period, Tommy Wilhelm leaned over in a friendly sort of way and told Joshua to meet him by the lower field at recess and they'd play soccer if it wasn't raining. And Rusty went with him to social studies so Joshua didn't have to walk down the corridor alone.

"Do you think Regan will tell the principal about the cigarette?" Rusty asked just loud enough to be heard by the fourth-grade girls walking ahead of them. They looked back at Joshua and giggled.

"Tell the principal?" Joshua asked, alarmed. "I never thought of that. Why would he?"

"Dunno," Rusty said. "You never know about Regan. He can be a grizzly."

"I hope he doesn't," Joshua said, following Rusty into the library, where social studies was held. "That would ruin my life."

Rusty shrugged. "Probably not ruin it completely."

In social studies Joshua couldn't concentrate on Russia. He didn't feel right. Not sick necessarily, but as if he might soon be sick. He was uncomfortable, aware of the way he looked in his father's huge shirt, how small his hands were, aware of his classmates watching him. They were probably thinking, "Joshua Bates is still stupid." He was afraid that the teacher, a tall stork of a woman with white feathery hair and a lisp, would recommend that he return to third grade because he couldn't concentrate on Russia.

He wondered if Mrs. Goodwin had heard about the cigarette. He certainly hoped she had not. He owed Mrs. Goodwin everything for helping him get promoted, teaching him to read and write and even spell, which he'd never been able to do. He couldn't bear to disappoint her. Before recess, he decided, he'd have to tell her that the cigarette was an accident, sort of a joke, that he hadn't meant to cause trouble.

And before he realized he had been daydreaming, drawing pictures of cats on his social studies notebook, the stork woman was standing right next to him at the library table.

"You are Joshua Bates. Correct?" she asked.

"Yes," Joshua said.

"I understand from Mrs. Goodwin that you did extremely well in third grade and have been promoted to our class."

Joshua nodded.

"That's very nice and we're pleased to have you," she said in her funny, floating voice. But she didn't sound very pleased at all. She sounded as if she was going to say something unpleasant, something critical, and suddenly Joshua imagined himself saying out loud in front of everybody, "Listen, bean brain. Tell the truth. You're not glad to see me at all."

In fact, he wondered if he *had* said it.

He checked her face for signs of anger.

"One of the rules in my class is to pay attention." She seemed to be screaming, her mouth opened wide in a birdlike yawn, her lips in an O. He was sure that the secretaries in the principal's office across the hall and even the principal could hear her shouting and would know that Joshua T. Bates was in trouble again.

"I don't expect you to know about Russian history since you just arrived, but I expect you to listen," the stork woman said.

"I was listening," Joshua said. "I was listening hard."

"I beg your pardon?" she asked.

"I said I was listening."

He shouldn't have said that, of course. He should have nodded and smiled and said he was sorry to have fallen into a daydream in her class. But he didn't and suddenly the stork woman seemed to expand like an angry bird, growing and growing until she looked to him as if she were filling the entire library with her bad temper.

When the bell rang for recess, Joshua followed Rusty out of the classroom.

"Is that what she's always like?" he asked Rusty.

"Miss Perry?" Rusty shrugged. "She likes girls better than boys," he said. "Tomorrow, come in a dress."

"Right," Joshua said, stopping by Mrs. Goodwin's classroom. "I'll borrow one of Amanda's." He laughed. But he was not really amused. In fact, he felt terrible and wanted to go home. "See you later," he called, watching Rusty fling his arm over Ethan's shoulder and head to the playground.

Joshua needed to talk to Mrs. Goodwin. He desperately needed to talk to her right away, but when he looked through the glass window on the door to the classroom, there was another student standing beside her desk, a girl who seemed to be crying. He caught Mrs. Goodwin's attention and waved.

"Later," she called. "Maybe after school."

And Joshua felt his own eyes fill with tears.

Every school day since the beginning of his second time in third grade, he had been with Mrs. Goodwin, her special project, her best student, her pride and joy. They had worked hours and hours together after school at her house, talked before school and after school and during recess. Anytime he needed her, she was there. Joshua came first before anyone else.

For a moment he watched her talk to the little girl with short brown curls rubbing her eyes. That was the way Mrs. Goodwin was—nothing mushy, no hugging or kissing or "I'm so sorry." She just listened and talked. It broke his heart to see her talking to someone else the way she had always talked to him.

He checked the clock over the library door. Already he was ten minutes late to meet up with Tommy Wilhelm, so he rushed down the hall to his locker, took out his jacket and Redskins cap, and ran down the back stairs out onto the playground.

Douglas Baer was at the bottom of the steps leaning against the school building just above the playing fields, looking off into the middle distance.

"Have you seen Tommy?" Joshua asked.

Douglas pointed in the direction of the lower field.

"Playing soccer," Douglas said. "Most of the fourth-grade boys are down there."

"Are you coming?" Joshua asked.

"Tommy didn't ask me," Douglas said.

"Do you have to be invited to play soccer at recess?" Joshua said.

"That's the way it is in fourth grade," Douglas said. "Tommy Wilhelm's in charge."

"Why don't you come with me?" Joshua asked.

"No, thanks," Douglas said. "I hate Tommy Wilhelm."

Joshua shrugged. He knew exactly how Douglas

felt. He remembered very well what it was like to be left out, and he still worried about it now, worried about it always.

He headed down the hill to the lower field where Tommy Wilhelm and a lot of the fourth-grade boys were playing soccer.

"Did you see Douglas?" Ethan asked, coming up behind Joshua.

"Yeah," Joshua said. "Up by the steps."

"Mad?" Ethan asked.

"He seemed sad," Joshua said.

"He's on Tommy's wrong side," Ethan said, hurrying down the hill with Joshua.

"How come?" Joshua said, although he certainly knew what it was like to be on Tommy Wilhelm's wrong side.

"Tommy's decided that Douglas is a nerd," Ethan said. "I don't know why. Douglas is my fourth best friend." He looked over at Joshua. "Actually, you're my fourth best friend and Douglas is my fifth."

And he ran onto the field, taking a place on Tommy Wilhelm's defense playing against the fifth grade.

Joshua waited. He didn't ask to play but stood on the sidelines hoping to be asked. Nothing happened. Tommy Wilhelm didn't even seem to notice him, although Ethan called out, "Joshua can play fullback."

But Joshua wasn't asked to play fullback. So he stood on one foot and then the other, his hands in the pockets of his ski jacket, waiting for the bell to signal the end of recess.

Maybe Tommy had decided he was a nerd again. Maybe Tommy had already forgotten how cool he thought it was for Joshua to come to school with a cigarette behind his ear. Maybe he'd forgotten that after math class he'd asked Joshua to meet him on the lower field.

Joshua was beginning to feel the way he had when he was held back in third grade.

"Weak is how I feel," he'd told his mother.

If Andrew were there instead of at home sick, then things would be different. If he were there standing at the edge of the soccer field with Joshua, he would say, "So what?"

"If Tommy doesn't like me," Joshua would say, "nobody will."

"Don't worry so much about what Tommy thinks, Josh," Andrew would say. "He's a bully."

"That's what my mother says."

"Mine too," Andrew would say.

Joshua knew that Andrew worried, too. Once last year Tommy wrote CHICKEN in chalk on the back of Andrew's jacket without his knowing and all through math everybody in the third grade but Andrew knew and didn't tell him. Not even Joshua. That's how it was with Tommy Wilhelm in charge of the class.

That afternoon walking home together, Joshua's arm slung over Andrew's shoulder, commiserating with his best friend, Andrew had said, "I wish Tommy Wilhelm would disappear."

"Me too," Joshua said.

"At least I wish there was something we could do so he wasn't so powerful," Andrew had said.

"Like what?"

Andrew shrugged. "Like I don't know. Maybe ignore him."

"We could try that tomorrow," Joshua said.

But it was difficult to ignore Tommy Wilhelm.

When the bell rang, Joshua was the first up the hill, passing Mr. Regan and Douglas Baer talking at the bottom of the steps, rushing two stairs at a time to his locker.

"So did you get to play?" Douglas asked, coming up the corridor just as Joshua opened his locker.

"Nope," Joshua said.

"I didn't think you would," Douglas said.

With a familiar sense of failure, Joshua hung up his jacket, took out his book bag with his library book and notebook for writing compositions, and some M & M's that Amanda had given him that morning.

"I don't much like soccer anyway," Joshua said to Douglas, and headed down the corridor to homeroom, where English class was held.

Chapter Five

Joshua walked home from school alone. The air smelled like rain and already it was getting dark even though it wasn't yet four o'clock, too dark to stop by Andrew's house to tell him about the miseries of fourth grade.

When he got home, he let himself in the back door and listened for his mother.

The house was too quiet. He didn't even hear the sweet sounds of Georgie chattering to herself or the hum of the washing machine. No one seemed to be there except Plutarch, who was sleeping on the table next to a note from Joshua's mother:

I'VE TAKEN GEORGIE TO THE DR. FOR HER CHECKUP, THEN TO THE MARKET, THEN HOME AT 6. I HOPE YOU LOVED 4TH GRADE, J.

LOVE, M.

Joshua dropped the note into the wastebasket and checked the fridge. It was empty except for pickles, mustard, olives, strawberry jam, a half-eaten container of raspberry yogurt, and leftover pot roast from the night before. There was no milk and no orange juice. There hadn't been any cookies in the red jar on the kitchen counter since Saturday, and the only fruit was a single brown squishy banana.

Sinking into the rocking chair next to the telephone, Joshua dialed Andrew's number.

"H'lo," he said. "This is Joshua Bates."

"Of course I know who it is," Mrs. Porter said. "How was your first day in fourth grade?"

"Great," Joshua lied. "Really great."

Why bother Mrs. Porter with bad news?

He had in mind to tell Andrew the truth, but Mrs. Porter said how sorry she was that Andrew couldn't come to the phone. He had strep throat and bronchitis and a fever and was too sick to lift his head off the pillow. Mrs. Porter, who was a doctor, was like that.

"Will he be in school tomorrow?" Joshua asked.

"I don't believe he'll be in school all week," Mrs. Porter said. "He's really quite ill."

Joshua's heart fell.

"And he won't be able to talk on the phone either?" he asked.

"Not today," Mrs. Porter said. "Not until his fever breaks. Is there anything I can tell him?"

"Nope," Joshua said. "Nothing."

He replaced the receiver and went into the living room.

He wasn't allowed to watch television on weekdays, but he turned on the television anyway and fell onto the couch, switching channels from one to the next, but there was nothing worth watching, nothing to take his mind off his terrible day.

So he flung his book bag over his shoulder, picked up Plutarch in his arms, and went upstairs to his room, falling facedown onto his bed, burrowing his face in his pillow.

Which is how Amanda found him when she appeared at his bedroom door.

"Hi," she said. "I didn't hear you come home."

Joshua turned over onto his back.

"I didn't know you were here either," he said, sitting up and turning on the light so he could see his sister standing at the foot of his bed.

She looked entirely different from how she had looked that morning as she got onto the bus to Alice Deal Junior High. She had on the lipstick and dangly earrings and nail polish that she had removed at her parents' request, but the real difference was her hair. It

seemed, in the filtered light of his bedroom, to be the color of purple grapes.

"Don't say anything," Amanda said. "I know already."

"What did you do?" Joshua asked.

Amanda reached up and touched her short purple bangs.

"Dyed it," she said. She sat down at the end of Joshua's bed. "Don't ask me why I dyed it."

Joshua shrugged. "Okay," he said. "I won't."

"The thing is," said the formerly brilliant Amanda Bates, Queen Mean of Lowell Street, looking as if she was going to cry, "all the girls in the seventh grade decided to dye their hair just a little. But not like this. Not purple."

"Maybe you can wash it out," Joshua said.

"I tried." Amanda shook her head. "It doesn't wash out."

"Brother," Joshua said, pulling Plutarch onto his lap. "Things have really gotten weird in our family this year."

"I know," Amanda said. "I sort of liked it better last year when I was smart and you were happy."

"Who wouldn't?" Joshua said.

For the first time ever, at least the first time since he could remember, Joshua felt terrible for his sister. They

43

had never been friends, not really friends, not since they were little. Amanda had been smart and good and obedient, the pride of the Bates family. At least that is the way she had been at Mirch Elementary. And Joshua had been "all boy"—so his father said—slow in school and a little bored, kept after classes for interrupting—not bad but not good, either. He was certainly not going to receive the Good Citizenship award, which Amanda had done.

He regarded Amanda's hair.

"Maybe what you should do is dye it another color—like your own color," he said.

"Brown?" she asked.

"Sort of dark brown," he said.

"Maybe I should get some dark brown dye before Mommy gets home." She turned to leave. "Daddy's going to kill me."

"I'll go with you," Joshua said.

It was dark by the time they left to go to the drugstore. They walked silently down Lowell Street toward Connecticut Avenue, but there was a warm feeling of friendship between them, a sense of danger in the darkness, a feeling of dependence on each other.

"So," Amanda said finally. "How was today?"

Joshua thought for a moment, wondering if he

should tell her what had really happened or if she would tell on him as she had always done last year and the year before and the year before that. Maybe he could tell her some of what had happened. Not all. Not about the cigarette.

"I had a terrible day today," he said. "I walked into the fourth-grade classroom, and guys were drawing these stupid pictures of teachers on the blackboard and they asked me to do one and I did."

And he told Amanda about the goons and the trouble that seemed to occur wherever he happened to be.

"Things are different than they were last year when all the grownups liked me," Amanda said matter-of-factly.

"I know," Joshua said. "Last year you wouldn't have dyed your hair, because of what the grownups would say."

"I don't like grownups as much as I used to," she said.

She turned to Joshua and brushed his shoulder with her own. "And I didn't used to like you," she said.

Joshua's heart filled.

If she didn't used to like him, that meant she did like him now. Which pleased Joshua very much.

They crossed the street and went into the drug-store, heading straight for the hair products aisle.

"Did you see who I saw?" Amanda asked when they stopped in front of the dyes.

"Nope," Joshua said.

"Tommy Wilhelm," she said.

"Smoking in front of the drugstore?"

"Nope," Amanda said. "Standing by the comic books."

At the drugstore they chose a color called sable, and Amanda picked up a new hairbrush and Joshua got a package of peanut M & M's, which he deserved since there was no food in the house.

When they got in line to pay, they saw Tommy at the counter with Billy Nickel, buying his comics.

"So," Tommy said. "What are you doing here?"

"Not much," Joshua said.

"How come your hair looks purple?" Billy Nickel asked Amanda.

"Because it *is* purple, bean brain," Amanda said in a perfectly pleasant voice, taking an M & M from Joshua's open bag.

"Purple," Tommy said. "Yuck."

"See you later," Joshua called as they left the store.

"Tommy Wilhelm's a disaster," Amanda said, walking up Lowell Street.

"I know," Joshua said. "But he happens to be the most important person in the fourth grade."

*　　*　　*

When Joshua and Amanda arrived home, they could see Mrs. Bates was cooking dinner. "Hi, guys," she called to them.

"I'm going straight up to the bathroom and get rid of the purple," Amanda whispered to Joshua. "You go in and talk to her."

"Hi, Mom," Joshua said.

He went into the kitchen, took off his jacket, and hung it on a hook by the back door.

"Andrew called," his mother said.

Joshua's heart leaped.

"I thought he was too sick to talk," he said. "That's what his mother told me."

Mrs. Bates smiled. "Andrew said to call in a hurry. His mother's gone to the grocery store."

So Joshua ran upstairs into Amanda's empty room and dialed Andrew. He didn't want his mother to hear his conversation.

"It was terrible," Joshua said when Andrew asked him about fourth grade. "Everything I did was wrong."

And he told Andrew about the cigarette and the goon picture and the math quiz and daydreaming in social studies and standing on the sidelines during the soccer game.

"I hate it," he said to Andrew.

"I know," Andrew said. "I wish I was going to be at school tomorrow."

"So do I," Joshua said. "What I wish is that I had something that made me feel different. Sort of bigger than I am."

"Like what?"

"I don't know. Tommy came to school in his older brother's basketball jacket today. Something like that."

"The thing is, you have to *feel* bigger," Andrew said.

"But I don't," Joshua said, lying on his back on Amanda's bed, his feet on the wall. Plutarch, who had followed him upstairs from the kitchen, kneaded his paws on Joshua's belly. "I just don't."

"Maybe," Andrew began, but his mother must have walked in the front door with the groceries, because he said he had to get off the telephone and would try to call Joshua if he had another chance.

Joshua lay on Amanda's bed thinking. In the bathroom next door he could hear the water running in the shower, so Amanda must be dyeing her hair sable brown. Downstairs his mother was singing in the kitchen, happily making supper, feeding Georgianna, and he thought he heard his father's car in front of the house.

He was remembering his father's Swiss Army

knife. Joshua admired the knife. It had every kind of tool—bottle opener, scissors, screwdriver, compass, and a magnifying glass—all neatly hidden in a sleek red container. It was kept in a cigar box with loose change and paper clips and thumbtacks in the top drawer of his father's bureau. His father took the knife on camping trips, and he had allowed Joshua to use it for opening bottles or fixing the flashlight.

It occurred to him that he would like to take the knife to school. Just slip it in his pocket and carry it around at school for a day or two. He knew of course that he shouldn't take a knife to school. Knives were not permitted at Mirch Elementary, and besides, his father would never allow him to borrow his Swiss Army knife, for reasons of safety. So that meant Joshua would have to take it from his father's bureau. Steal it.

He listened for his father at the front door and didn't hear the door open. He looked out Amanda's window and under the streetlight saw his father outside with the trunk open, looking for something.

Quickly he tiptoed into his parents' room, over to his father's bureau. He opened the top drawer, opened the cigar box, and there was the Swiss Army knife just as he expected. Then he closed the cigar box, closed the drawer, went into his own room, and turned on the light just as his mother called him for dinner.

＊　　＊　　＊

Amanda was at the kitchen table with a towel stained brown around her head. Joshua slipped into a chair beside her.

"She knows," Amanda said. "She came upstairs and saw me."

"I'd have to be color blind not to know, darling," Mrs. Bates said.

"But don't make a big deal about it in front of Daddy," Amanda said just as Mr. Bates walked in the front door calling "Hello, hello," kissing his wife, his children, and handing Joshua an envelope with his name on it.

"This was stuck in the front door," his father said, tousling Joshua's hair, asking him about his first day in fourth grade.

"It was great," Joshua said, full of trepidation as he opened the envelope.

"Really great?" Mrs. Bates asked. "I'm so glad, darling."

"Sort of great," Joshua said.

The note was brief, written in pencil and unsigned. It said:

WELCOME BACK TO THE 3RD GRADE, JOSHUA BATES.

Joshua folded the note quickly and put it into his pocket.

"Who's that from?" Amanda asked.

"Somebody you don't know," Joshua said, picking at his pasta, too nervous to eat.

Chapter Six

Joshua barely slept all night. For a long time he lay in bed in the dark looking at the ceiling, watching the headlights from traffic on Thirty-fourth Street slide up his wall. At one fifteen by the alarm clock next to his bed, he got up and turned on his light.

The note was from Tommy Wilhelm. Joshua was sure of it. He took it out of the drawer of his desk where he'd put it after dinner and looked at it under the light. It was written in pencil in bold print except for the Joshua Bates on the envelope. That was written in thin squiggly dancing lines as if the writer were ridiculing Joshua in his handwriting. The note was un-signed. But of course Tommy had written it. He had probably written it when Joshua and Amanda saw him at the pharmacy. No doubt Tommy and Billy Nickel had gone outside the pharmacy to have their usual cig-arette and Tommy had written the note and then the two of them had walked up the dark streets to Lowell Street, slipped the note in the Bateses' front door, and headed north to Tommy's house on Cathedral Avenue, probably laughing all the way, planning a terrible day on Tuesday at Mirch Elementary for Joshua Bates.

Outside his bedroom door Plutarch was sleeping stretched out on the rug belly-up. When Joshua peered into Amanda's room with the unlikely hope that she had insomnia as well, he saw she was sleeping on her stomach, a pillow over her head. His parents' door was closed. He didn't want to turn on any lights in the hall in case his parents did wake up. Then he would have to explain to them why he couldn't sleep. So he walked downstairs in the dark. He walked through the living room, which was alive with the sounds of an old house, the rattle of radiators, the creaking of the wood floors, sounds he couldn't determine, which seemed to be coming from the basement, his least favorite part of the house even in daylight. He went into the kitchen, got a package of chocolate chip cookies, and sat down at the kitchen table in the dark, only the silver half moon lighting the night outside the window. He ate the cookies one after the other until almost half the package was gone and he felt a little woozy.

He was thinking about tomorrow.

In September, when Joshua had been held back in the third grade, he made serious plans to run away to East Africa. Now that he knew something about Africa, including how long a trip it would be to get there, it seemed unlikely that he would be going. Not even to Michigan where his aunt and uncle lived or Connecticut where his grandparents were. Somehow he was going to have to find a way to be in the fourth grade at Mirch Elementary as a perfectly normal boy without the number of troubles he now had. Which would not be easy as long as Tommy Wilhelm was alive and living in Washington.

He thought about the knife. At first he thought about the knife itself, how it looked in the cigar box, red and shiny and important, and how it felt to hold it, a fat but not large knife, compact, efficient. He liked the feel of it in his hand.

As he finished the chocolate chip cookies, which then sat in a sugar mountain at the bottom of his stomach, he imagined the knife in his pocket as he walked to school, weighting the bottom of it, resting there during homeroom and first period and second period, while Tommy Wilhelm and Billy Nickel organized their humiliation of Joshua T. Bates. And then it would be recess, time for soccer, time for Tommy to choose the people worthy of playing with him. Joshua wouldn't be one of them. But he'd be there, probably standing with Douglas Baer on the sidelines, and he'd take the Swiss Army knife out of his pocket.

"Have you seen one of these?" he'd ask Douglas Baer.

"I don't think so," Douglas would say.

"Let me show you," Joshua would say, and he'd begin to open the compartments, the scissors, the bottle opener, the compass, finally the blades, a tiny one, then a larger one, and then quite a wide, significant-looking blade with a very sharp edge.

By the time the Swiss Army knife was open to show all of its wonderful parts, the boys on the soccer field would have gathered around him in a tight group, no room for Tommy Wilhelm to get close to the knife. Poor Tommy and his sidekick Billy Nickel left out of the circle in which Joshua was the one in charge.

It was almost three A.M. when Joshua went upstairs, checked Plutarch still sleeping on the floor in the hall, checked Amanda, who had turned over onto her back, checked Georgianna, who was snoring a small baby-sounding snore, and climbed into his own bed, where he might have fallen asleep for just a moment before morning but didn't remember it.

Joshua was up and dressed before anyone else in his family, dressed in the same clothes he had worn on Monday and sitting at his desk doing his math homework.

He heard Amanda in the bathroom, probably examining her expressions in the mirror, heard the cheerful sounds of Georgianna and his mother downstairs in the kitchen cooking breakfast. It smelled like oatmeal, which he hated. He listened for his father, listened carefully, and then heard him walk out of his bedroom, say something to Amanda, greet Plutarch, and go down the stairs.

Joshua didn't think about the knife now. He had done all of his thinking the night before, sitting in the kitchen in the dark. He got up from his desk, checked the bathroom door, which was closed, went through the door into his parents' room, opened the dresser, opened the cigar box, took his father's fine red knife, and dropped it into his pocket, where it felt huge, the size of a basketball.

Then he went back into his bedroom, closed his math book, packed his book bag, and went downstairs for breakfast, sitting across the table from his father and hoping his father couldn't see the stolen knife in Joshua's pocket with his electric-blue x-ray eyes.

On the way to the bus with Amanda, Joshua wanted to tell her what he had done. He was excited and terrified at once. Excited for the feeling of importance the knife gave him, even now, walking along Lowell Street with an invisible object in his pocket. And he was terrified because he had stolen from his father and was on his

way to school with something illegal in his pocket. But the feelings of terror and excitement were somehow the same. They both made his heart beat faster, his blood run hotter in his body, his breath come thinner in his chest.

Joshua knew he could be in terrible trouble this time.

If he told Amanda what he had done, there would be two of them involved in the stealing. Although she had not been the one to take the knife, she would know about it and he wouldn't be all alone with the danger.

But Amanda left him no room to talk. She was in a miserable humor. Her hair had not turned out to be sable brown but a sort of sick shade of dark purple after all the dyeing. Their father was furious and had recommended that she change junior high schools, perhaps go to a Catholic school where the standards for dress were blue uniforms and no makeup. She had not finished her biology homework and had lost her English exercises in vocabulary, for which she would probably receive an F. Not her first F this year, either. Their parents didn't even know about the first one, since that F, in math, would appear on her next report card. Besides that, their mother wasn't going to let her spend the night at Tina Song's house this weekend, claiming Tina Song was a bad influence and did not have proper parental supervision. So she was planning to go without their permission.

By the time Amanda got on the bus, Joshua felt much better in comparison to his sister. Almost good.

Tommy Wilhelm was sitting alone on the front steps when Joshua walked up the sidewalk toward Mirch Elementary. Joshua hoped Tommy hadn't seen him so he could go around the side of the school and begin the day without a conversation with Tommy. But it was too late.

"Did you get my note?" Tommy asked as Joshua walked by.

"Nope," Joshua said. "I didn't."

Tommy frowned. "Billy put it in your front door," he said.

"Well, it wasn't there," Joshua said. "Maybe he forgot." The lie came easily, surprising him. He didn't used to lie until lately.

He went up the steps past Tommy and through the front door, arriving at his locker at the same time as Douglas Baer, three lockers down.

"Do you like fourth grade better than third?" Douglas asked.

Joshua shrugged. He opened his locker and hung up his jacket, opened his book bag and took out his library book and math book for first period.

"It's sort of the same," Joshua said.

"Except for Tommy," Douglas said, leaning against the lockers, waiting for Joshua to go to homeroom.

"I thought everybody liked Tommy," Joshua said.

"Maybe. My father says they don't like him. They're scared of him," Douglas said. "I hate him."

"Yeah," Joshua said.

"You hate him too?" Douglas asked, walking down the corridor with Joshua, past the library, the all-purpose room, past Mrs. Goodwin's third grade.

"Not exactly," Joshua said, following Douglas into homeroom.

"You should. He wouldn't let you play soccer yesterday and he probably won't let you today. He has too much control."

"I know," Joshua said. "It's weird we let him be in charge like that."

He opened his library book and pretended to read.

Joshua was nervous. He liked the feel of the Swiss Army knife in his pocket. It made him feel important and strong and powerful. But now that he was at school, in the building with all of the teachers and the librarian and the principal, he was especially aware that he was breaking the rules. Knives were not allowed. They were not merely against the rules like water guns and candy and matches. They were a serious offense.

And Joshua was suddenly afraid that the knife might show before he got to the playground at recess, might be sticking out of his pocket so Mr. Regan could see it clearly and identify it as a knife. But he didn't want to check and call attention to the knife, which felt huge and heavy, weighing down his pocket. Contraband, a serious crime.

When Billy Nickel arrived in the classroom, Joshua tried to burrow his head in his library book, but Billy saw him and walked straight over to his seat, Tommy Wilhelm right behind him, and asked if he didn't find the note in his door.

"Nope," Joshua said.

He was not going to let his two enemies know the truth. He wasn't going to give them the satisfaction. He was glad he'd left the note at home in the top drawer of his desk.

"I put it there last night before I went home for dinner," Billy said. Joshua could tell that Billy was afraid of Tommy, too, afraid that Tommy would be angry at him for not carrying out orders, for lying.

"Well, I can't help it. It wasn't there," Joshua said, hoping very much that Billy wouldn't tell him in public, in front of all his new classmates in the fourth grade, what the note had said.

Mr. Regan was in a bad humor. He told the class they'd have to work hard and behave themselves and get their work in on time and not whisper back and forth in class, because he'd been up all night with his wife, who was having a baby, and the baby might come any minute and he was a wreck.

In the seat next to Joshua, Tommy rolled his eyes.

But math class passed quickly without a quiz. Mr. Regan explained fractions and assigned exercises to be completed while he went to the principal's office to telephone his wife.

While Mr. Regan was out of the room, Tommy Wilhelm leaned over toward Joshua to look at his paper.

"I better not cheat off your paper or I'll flunk," he said in a loud voice.

And all the boys in the class laughed. Except Douglas Baer.

In social studies, the stork lady showed a film about Russia under the Soviets. With the lights off in the all-purpose room, Joshua fell asleep for most of the movie since he'd been up half the night.

And then the bell rang for recess.

Today Joshua was in a hurry. He wasn't going to

stop by Mrs. Goodwin's room to talk to her this morning. He wanted to get straight to the playground, to the lower field where the soccer games took place, even though Tommy Wilhelm hadn't asked him to play as he had the day before. Joshua ran down the steps, just behind Rusty, and onto the playing field.

Douglas Baer was standing with a new boy in the fourth grade and some of the girls. He called to Ethan, but Ethan didn't reply.

"Remember yesterday I told you Douglas was my fifth best friend?" Ethan asked Joshua, hurrying along beside him.

"I remember," Joshua said.

"Well, he's not," Ethan said seriously. "He's not any number. Who is *your* best friend?"

"Andrew," Joshua said.

"Oh, Andrew," Ethan said. "He's okay but kind of a nerd."

"Not if you get to know him," Joshua said defensively.

Joshua wasn't asked to play soccer. He stood on the sidelines, rubbing his hands together because the day was cold and damp to the bone.

He was not surprised that he hadn't been asked to play. It was exactly what he had expected. Tommy Wilhelm wanted him back in the third grade. That's what

the note said. Of course he wasn't going to be invited to play with the fourth-grade boys.

Later when Joshua thought about it, he knew he was not exactly trying to show off by taking the knife out of his pocket, opening all of the blades and the bottle opener and the scissors and the compass and the magnifying glass. He had planned to take the knife out so the boys in his class, especially Tommy, would know he had a knife, but he hadn't planned to open it. In his daydreams of this moment, the knife was closed.

But he was trying to pretend it did not matter a bit to him to be standing on the sidelines as if he were invisible. And so after he took the knife out of his pocket and held it in his hand admiring its sleek red case, he opened it.

When the warning bell for the end of recess rang and the boys playing soccer on the field filed by him, they stopped to watch. They watched him close it, blade by blade, the scissors, the magnifying glass, the compass.

"Awesome," Ethan said. "Where'd you get it?"

"For my birthday," Joshua said, lying easily. But his heart caught in his throat because he hadn't planned to lie, had not planned to be asked where he got the knife. But the lie came to him like magic, without thinking. With a sudden sinking feeling, it occurred to him that maybe he was turning bad.

"Show me how it opens," Tommy Wilhelm asked.

Joshua pulled open the blades one by one.

"It's really amazing," Tommy said.

"Wild," Billy Nickel said.

"Watch out, guys," Ethan said. "There's Regan at the top of the hill on his way down to get us because we're late."

"Beat it on the double," Tommy called, sprinting up the hill.

Joshua closed the knife, stuffed it in the back pocket of his jeans, and ran up the hill after Tommy Wilhelm, past Douglas, who was standing near the gym with Brendan, and in the back door of Mirch Elementary.

"What do we have next period?" he asked Billy Nickel.

"English," Billy said. "We're reading *Charlotte's Web*, remember?"

Joshua opened his locker, hung up his jacket, took *Charlotte's Web* out of his book bag, and walked with Billy to homeroom.

It wasn't until he sat down at his desk in the back of the room that he was aware of a feeling that something was missing. He checked his books, his pencils, his notebook, and then he checked his pockets, reaching into the right back pocket where he'd put the knife. It was gone.

Chapter Seven

For the rest of the day, Joshua couldn't get his father's knife out of his mind. After school was over he searched the back field of the playground for the Swiss Army knife, but he couldn't find it. He found a quarter and a pink barrette and a doctor's excuse for Mary Marks to miss gym and a new baseball, but he couldn't find his father's knife even though he walked up and down the hill where he had lost it until a teacher came out and said that school was over and he had to go home.

Joshua walked home alone feeling miserable, wishing Andrew were there to talk to, or even Amanda, his new friend and formerly terrible sister. Anyone to help him, to talk about what he had done.

As he walked past Veazy Street where Andrew lived, his head down, his shoulders hunched against the cold, he checked his watch. It was late. He must have been on the playground searching for the knife for a very long time, because it was almost five o'clock, late for him to get home from school. But it was early for Andrew's mother and father to get home from work. And so he took a chance and walked three blocks to the brown brick house where Andrew lived. The Porters' blue Toyota station wagon was not in the driveway. The house was dark, or at least it seemed dark, with one light coming from the back, probably the kitchen. He walked up the long hill of steps and knocked on the door.

No one answered. Perhaps Mrs. Porter had taken Andrew to the doctor. He put his head against the front door and listened. He didn't hear anyone, but he had the sense that someone was there, so he knocked again.

"Who's there?" a woman's voice asked.

"Joshua."

"Joshua Bates?" It was Andrew's voice.

"Of course. It's not Joshua Salamander."

Andrew, in his pajamas and looking very white, was standing just behind the baby-sitter when she opened the door. Joshua stepped inside.

"You might get my sickness," Andrew said.

"I'd love to get your sickness," Joshua said. "Give it to me immediately."

He followed Andrew to the kitchen and sat down across from him at the large wooden table.

"So," Joshua said. "I'm in trouble again."

"Like what?"

"Like *real* trouble," Joshua said. "Like a crime."

And he told Andrew everything from the beginning. About the knife. About taking it from his father and taking it to school in the pocket of his jeans and onto the playground. About taking it out of his pocket and opening it, one blade after the other, and showing it to all of the fourth-grade boys. About losing it on the playground after recess.

"Brother," Andrew said. "You're not kidding about trouble."

"I know," Joshua said. "I'm really scared."

"So what do you think's going to happen?"

Joshua shook his head.

"You have to tell your father," Andrew said. "That's the first thing you have to do."

"I know," Joshua said. "It makes me sick just to think about it."

"And then I guess he'll help you if you're in big trouble at school."

"Maybe," Joshua said. "But what I'm hoping is that I'm not in big trouble at school. That no one will tell."

"But someone will hand the knife in to lost and found," Andrew said.

"Or else keep it," Joshua said.

"Steal it? I can't believe anybody at Mirch would steal like that," Andrew said.

"I can," Joshua said. "I did."

"I guess you did," Andrew said.

"What I really hope is that the knife was stolen from the playground and that I have enough money in the bank to buy my father a new one and put it back in the cigar box without his ever finding out."

"Right," Andrew said. "But it probably won't happen like that."

"Probably not," Joshua said.

Andrew checked the clock over the stove.

"You better go," he said. "My mother will be home from work pretty soon, and she won't be glad to see that you've come over when I'm supposedly dying."

It was almost completely dark when Joshua left, so he walked up to Wisconsin Avenue, where there was more traffic and more streetlights and more people walking along the avenue. He wished he had another best friend to visit. He didn't want to go home.

Usually Joshua was not afraid of the dark, particularly not at home and not walking along the streets at night, although he was seldom out alone after the sun went down. But tonight he was afraid. He felt as if something was going to happen. As if it *should* happen.

Some kind of punishment for what he had done. He found himself expecting someone to be hiding behind the trees that lined Wisconsin Avenue, lying in wait for him to pass; expecting a car to run off the road just where he was walking; expecting the police, who had been alerted to the fact that he was a criminal and on the loose. All along the way he either ran or walked quickly or looked behind him to see if someone was following.

It was only six o'clock when he arrived home. His father's car was already parked in front of the house, which meant trouble. It must mean trouble, he thought, since his father was never home before seven, usually seven thirty, just in time to eat dinner.

Just as he got to the front door, he heard a window open upstairs and Amanda stuck her head out.

"Josh," she called in a stage whisper.

"Is something the matter?" he asked. "Is that why Daddy's home?"

"Something *is* the matter," she said. "Maybe you should go to East Africa right away."

"Oh, great," Joshua said, his stomach falling. He was about to ask Amanda what had happened, but she shut the window and was gone.

Joshua took a deep breath, opened the front door, and went into the hall. He heard Georgianna chattering in the kitchen, heard his mother's voice, but no one called his name and he did not intend to announce his arrival. Amanda stood at the top of the stairs motioning to him to come up so she could tell him what had happened.

But it was too late.

"Joshua," Mr. Bates called from the kitchen. His voice was severe.

"Yes," Joshua said. He took off his jacket and hung it in the closet, tossed his cap on the shelf, and stuffed his gloves in the pockets of his jacket.

"Your mother and I are in the kitchen."

Great, Joshua thought. "Your mother and I"—that was not the usual way his father spoke to him, not formally, not severely.

His father, still in his business suit, with an unfriendly expression on his long angular face, was holding Georgianna.

"Sit down," his father said. "I have something to ask you."

"Okay," Joshua said, trying without success to look straight at his father.

"In the top drawer of my bureau I keep a knife," his father said.

Joshua was afraid he was going to be sick. He had the sense that his head was wobbling and might fall off. In fact he wished it would.

"I know," he said weakly.

"When I opened the drawer this evening, the knife had disappeared," his father said.

Joshua's mind was working quickly. "I don't know," he began. "I mean, I know you have a knife."

"I think you do know, Joshua," his father said. "Your mother received a call from your new fourth-grade teacher, who said that you had been playing with a Swiss Army knife on the playground." He lifted Georgianna off his lap and put her on the floor. "Apparently the knife fell out of your back pocket. One of the students picked it up and turned it in."

Joshua put his head on the table and closed his eyes.

"I feel sick," he said quietly.

"I expect you do," his father said.

"I think I have to go to bed," Joshua said, getting up from the table and dragging himself upstairs to his room.

"I'm really sorry," Amanda said, following Joshua into his bedroom.

"Maybe I'll explode," Joshua said, falling face-down onto his bed.

"I don't think so," Amanda said.

"Or disappear," Joshua said. "Were you here when Daddy found out?"

"I was. First he went into his room to check about

73

the knife and then he came into my room to talk about the sins of dyeing your hair. It's been a really fun evening."

"It was dumb. It was the stupidest thing I've ever done."

"I know," Amanda said.

"I can't even believe I was such an idiot," Joshua said. "If Daddy happens to come upstairs with the idea of having a conversation with me, please tell him I've thrown up thirty-one times and I'm asleep."

"Don't worry," Amanda said. "He'll come."

Joshua fell asleep but woke up when his father and mother came upstairs and sat on the bed. He was too tired and worried to talk, but they spoke to him warmly, asking him why he had taken the knife and why he had done such a thing as to take it to school.

"Mrs. Goodwin called and would like to talk to you before school tomorrow," his mother said.

"Great," Joshua said.

"And Joshua," his father said just before they left, "Mr. Barnes wants me to come in tomorrow morning so we can talk to him together."

"I don't want to talk to him," Joshua said.

"I'm sure you don't," his father said. "But he's the principal and you have to talk to him."

"What else do I have to do?" Joshua asked.

"I want to find out what happened today and why you felt it was necessary to take my knife to school," his father said.

"I hope you know I feel terrible about it," Joshua said.

"I do know that," his father replied.

"I thought I needed to have a knife at school today," Joshua said weakly. "I can't exactly explain why."

"Well, think about it," his father said.

"I will," Joshua said. "I promise." And he thought of nothing else, tossing and turning all night.

Chapter Eight

Joshua got up early and put on the same clothes he had worn the day before and the day before that. Then he packed his book bag, picked up Plutarch from under the covers where he was sleeping, and went downstairs before his parents were even dressed.

His plan was to leave quickly before anyone else was downstairs so he didn't have to have any more conversations with his father. If he ate breakfast in a flash, fed Plutarch, put out the trash—which was his job for the month of November—and left, he would be able to miss another talk with his father and would be in time to see Mrs. Goodwin before any other children arrived at school.

He left a note on the kitchen table—GONE TO SCHOOL EARLY TO SEE MRS. GOODWIN—and rushed out the back door just as he heard his father's voice in the upstairs hall.

Mrs. Goodwin was correcting papers at her desk when Joshua walked into her classroom at seven thirty, before any of the third graders had arrived at school, before the crossing guards were even in place.

She put away the papers, pulled up a chair for Joshua, shut the door to her classroom, and sat down beside him. He liked that Mrs. Goodwin listened to him intently, as though she had never until that moment had a more interesting or amusing or important companion than Joshua T. Bates. He liked especially that she didn't criticize. Which is not to say she thought everything that Joshua did or said was right. But she didn't tell him he was wrong. She listened and told stories and asked questions and questions and questions, which is what she did on this bright, sunny Wednesday morning.

"Last night as I walked home I was thinking about you and wondering why you came to school on your first day of fourth grade with a cigarette," she said, folding her arms across her chest.

"It was behind my ear," Joshua said.

"Yes, I heard it was behind your ear," she said.

"I mean, I wasn't planning to smoke it, of course," he said.

"Of course not," Mrs. Goodwin said.

"I was—I don't know." Joshua shrugged. "Feeling weird."

"Weird?" she asked.

"Small," he said. "I was feeling really small. And

77

Amanda told me that Tommy Wilhelm smokes cigarettes in front of the drugstore, so..." He shrugged again. "You know."

"There was a conversation about it yesterday at the teachers' meeting," Mrs. Goodwin said. "They asked me if you were in the habit of such things in third grade and I said no."

"They probably said something about my father's knife, too, didn't they?" Joshua said, slinking down in his chair.

"They didn't mention your father, but they did bring up the knife," Mrs. Goodwin said. "And by the time I got home last night, thinking of the cigarette and the knife, I remembered how helpful you were to me earlier this fall when Mr. Goodwin and I were getting a divorce and I was feeling terrible."

"I know," Joshua said.

"I wanted to thank you for that," Mrs. Goodwin said.

"S'okay," Joshua said.

Janie Sears knocked on the door to the classroom, and Mrs. Goodwin waved her in. Janie was followed by Sally Stone and Paulie Soll, and soon the room was full of Joshua's old classmates in third grade.

"Aren't you going to say something else?" Joshua asked.

"About what?" Mrs. Goodwin got up to walk with Joshua to the door.

"About the knife and stuff."

"Joshua, I know it has been very hard for you to go into the fourth grade in the middle of the year," Mrs. Goodwin said. "Which doesn't excuse what you did. Especially bringing a knife, which could be dangerous."

"I know," Joshua said.

"But you will have enough punishment for that, especially from yourself." And then she did something she had never done. She ruffled his hair as if he were a small boy. For a moment, half a second really, before he went into the hallway and joined the flood of fourth and fifth graders racing to class, he felt wonderful, incapable of trouble or bad behavior or bad grades.

When Joshua walked into homeroom just after the bell, there was an announcement on the blackboard.

MR. REGAN'S WIFE HAD A BABY GIRL,
SAMANTHA, 6 LBS. 4 OZS., 19"

Underneath the message about Mr. Regan's baby was written:

JOSHUA BATES, REPORT TO THE PRINCIPAL'S OFFICE
AFTER HOMEROOM.

Joshua took his place at his desk between Rusty's and Tommy Wilhelm's desks.

"What's that about?" Rusty asked Joshua.

Joshua shrugged.

He wasn't about to tell Rusty or Tommy Wilhelm, who was chewing bubble gum with his hand over his mouth so the substitute teacher couldn't see him.

"The substitute came in about ten minutes ago and wrote it on the board," Tommy Wilhelm said.

"So you should tell her you're Joshua Bates," Billy Nickel said. "And go find out what's up."

"I'll tell her," Joshua said.

"I hope you're not in trouble," Billy said.

"I'm sure I'm not," Joshua said, even though his stomach was doing flip-flops.

He didn't want to make a scene. He didn't want the substitute to say something to embarrass him in front of the class, and he didn't want anyone to know that he had lost his father's knife.

He was just making plans to be excused to go to the boys' room when the principal's secretary appeared like a long-winged vulture out of nowhere and called out so no one for miles around could miss what she said: "Joshua, your father is here, so come along now and meet Mr. Barnes in his office."

And then with a sweep of her large wings, she was out of the room and down the hall.

"Great," Joshua said.

He couldn't think of anything else to say like, "Great, I'm very glad. That should be a lot of fun," or "Great, that's the end of my life as an ordinary ten-year-old boy," or "Great, I'm looking forward to a week in jail to catch up on my vocabulary."

"What's up?" Tommy asked.

"Who knows?" Joshua said.

He walked down the corridor, past Douglas Baer running with his Russian project, late for homeroom, and Janie Sears on her way to the infirmary with chickenpox and Brendan struggling to stuff his book bag and a soccer ball into his locker.

Mr. Bates sat on the long brown couch in Mr. Barnes's office, his legs crossed at the knee, his red-striped tie a little crooked, his look stern, as it sometimes was when there was trouble.

"Hello, Joshua," he said in his low formal voice as if they were old acquaintances who had not seen each other for a long time.

"H'lo," Joshua said.

He wanted to put his head down so he didn't have to see his father and Mr. Barnes, so they didn't have to see him. He wanted to put his face on the beige carpeted floor of the principal's office and disappear. But he forced himself to meet his father's eyes, to look at Mr. Barnes straight on, although from his vantage point, he did not seem to have eyes, only pinpoints on either side of his nose, above his mustache.

"I missed you this morning," his father said.

"I had to get to school early," Joshua said, "so I could get to my appointment with Mrs. Goodwin before classes started."

He wished his mother were sitting there in her blue skirt and soft white sweater, maybe holding Georgianna, who would be cooing softly, eating a banana. But his mother wasn't there and it was clear she was not coming. Only Mr. Bates and Mr. Barnes and Joshua, and pretty soon the missing Swiss Army knife was going to be there, too.

"As I told you last night, we're here about the knife," his father said.

"Right," Joshua said.

He meant Wrong. Wrong, he took the knife. Wrong, he brought it to school. Wrong, he'd lied. Had he lied? He couldn't remember. So many things had happened since yesterday.

"Why don't you tell Mr. Barnes what happened," his father said.

Joshua didn't want to tell Mr. Barnes what happened. The knife wasn't his business. It was his father's knife and his father's business, and even though it made Joshua feel very sick, he was willing to talk to his father about the knife. But not Mr. Barnes.

Mr. Barnes took the knife out of his drawer and put it on top of a stack of papers and children's drawings on his crowded desk.

"Billy Nickel found this knife yesterday and turned it in," Mr. Barnes said. "You know that."

"No," Joshua said. "I didn't know that."

"Well, that's what happened," Mr. Barnes said. "He found the knife on the playground and brought it to the office and said he had seen you with it on the playground during recess and guessed it must have fallen out of your pocket."

Joshua looked at him without speaking.

"So I called your house last night and spoke with your father and we arranged to meet with you today before language arts," Mr. Barnes said.

"I'm not going to talk about the knife," Joshua said. "I can't."

And that was true. Somehow he could not or would not talk about the knife. The words were caught in his throat, out of terror or shame or anger. It was as though he had lockjaw on the subject of the knife.

And that is the way the meeting went. Joshua would not talk about the knife and no one, not his father or Mr. Barnes, could make him. Mr. Barnes spoke about knives and their great danger to children, about obedience and rules, about social adjustment and good schools and disciplined behavior.

Joshua sat on the couch with his arms folded across his chest and would not speak.

When the bell finally rang, he got up.

"I have to go to class," he said, walking out of the office, his heart beating like crazy. He hurried down the hallway, past the library, past Mrs. Goodwin's third grade, and ducked into the boys' room.

Chapter Nine

He sat on the toilet in a stall with the door hooked and his knees up so no one could see his feet under the door and identify his black hightops with the red laces. Sitting on the toilet seat with his feet up, he had plenty of time to think.

He thought about friends and who, besides Andrew, he could count on to be a friend. He thought about Billy Nickel turning the Swiss Army knife in to the principal, just when Joshua was thinking that he had impressed Billy Nickel and they could become friends.

Tommy Wilhelm came in the boys' room and called him.

"The fourth-grade substitute wants to find you, Joshua, wherever you are," he said.

But Joshua said nothing, and Tommy didn't bother to check the toilet stalls.

Rusty came in with Ethan, and they talked about

Joshua, never imagining that he could hear everything they had to say.

"What's up with Joshua Bates?" That was Rusty's voice.

"Dunno," Ethan said. "He's in some kind of trouble."

"Did you see his father?"

"Yes, of course. Everyone saw him."

"My father's never been called into the school," Rusty said.

"Mine either," Ethan said. "Poor Joshua. Just when he gets promoted."

"I like him this year," Rusty said. "He used to be sort of a nerd, but he's getting better."

"Yeah," Ethan said, and they left then, padding across the floor and out the door.

So he'd been a nerd in third grade. That surprised him. He thought he'd been regular, like Andrew, although not as smart. But maybe Andrew was a nerd, too.

Sometimes Joshua didn't like to be young—at least as young as ten years old. Too many other people had control of his life. Teachers and parents and other people's parents and principals and teenagers and librarians. There was nothing he could do without asking.

But the worst part of being young, he decided as he sat on the toilet seat picking a scab on his knee through the hole in his jeans, until it bled, were the kids his own age.

Life had been easy when he was small, before he went to kindergarten, when his mother and father thought he was good and smart and funny. But the older he got in school, the more trouble he was to his parents and the more careful he had to be about the way he dressed and talked and walked and what he did after school and who his friends were and what he liked on television and what he liked in the movies and what he liked in sports.

He was so busy being somebody else, somebody that Tommy Wilhelm might like, that he was even beginning to forget who he was—Joshua T. Bates—an ordinary boy. Not ordinary exactly, because he had extraordinary daydreams of photographing wild animals in East Africa—zebras and tigers and giraffes—like the ones he'd seen on television programs. And he liked to watch television with his mother and father, sitting between them so their shoulders touched his. He still liked to have his mother read to him. And he liked to dress up and go out to dinner and drink Sprite from a wineglass and order portobello mushrooms and, later, chocolate mousse for dessert. These were not things an ordinary boy was supposed to like. These were secrets he kept from his friends, because he wanted to be thought of as a perfectly regular member of the group. And mostly he was.

But the group wasn't even a very good group, he thought. Not with Tommy Wilhelm in charge of the way a fourth-grade boy was supposed to be.

When the bell for recess rang, he unlocked the stall and went out. Billy Nickel was combing his hair in the mirror and Brendan was sitting on the floor putting on his sneakers.

"Where were you?" Brendan asked. "Everyone was looking for you."

"Here," Joshua said.

"How come?" Billy Nickel asked.

"Because I wanted to be," Joshua said.

"Your father was looking for you, too," Brendan said.

"Is he still here?" Joshua asked.

"Dunno," Brendan said. "But I know he gave a note to the substitute."

"Great," Joshua said.

"And he's coming back at lunchtime."

"Double great," Joshua said.

Brendan looked up. "Are you in trouble?"

"Nope," Joshua said, but he wasn't going to continue the conversation. He left the boys' room, walked down the corridor, and was very pleased to see that

Mrs. Goodwin was sitting alone in her classroom eating a pear.

"Hi," Joshua said, walking into the room.

"Hello, Joshua," Mrs. Goodwin said, splitting the pear in half, giving Joshua the other half. "It's a little messy," she said. "If I had a knife, I could do this more easily."

"Oh, well." Joshua shrugged. "I left my knife in the principal's office."

Mrs. Goodwin smiled. "That's what your father said a little while ago. He told me if I saw you to tell you he'd like to meet you here for lunch."

"In the cafeteria?" Joshua asked. That was the last thing he needed. His father in the cafeteria.

"He's planning to take you out to lunch, he said." Mrs. Goodwin put her chin in her hands and looked at Joshua. "I saw him this morning after he met with you in Mr. Barnes's office."

"So he told you about that," Joshua said.

"He did."

"I couldn't talk to Mr. Barnes. I couldn't say a word. Did he tell you that?" Joshua asked.

"He didn't," Mrs. Goodwin said. "But I don't blame you. You were too worried to talk."

"Right," Joshua said. "But I don't get too worried when I'm around you."

"And you shouldn't get worried around your father, either," Mrs. Goodwin said.

"I don't usually, I guess," Joshua said. "But this has been a big thing."

His father was a little late. Joshua was waiting on the front steps of Mirch Elementary when he drove up in the red Jeep and gave a little cheerful beep.

He had picked up lunch at the deli near his office, tuna salad sandwiches and sodas and potato chips, not the usual Mirch cafeteria school lunch, and they drove around the block into the parking lot behind a bank to eat.

Mr. Bates was in a good humor and Joshua was glad for that. He patted Joshua's knee and told him a joke about a snake and a tiger and told him the family might go to New York City for New Year's Eve. He talked about sports and how maybe they'd get some Orioles tickets for next summer. He didn't even mention the knife until they had finished eating and he had checked his watch.

"In a few minutes I have to get you back to school," he said. "And I wanted to say something to you. I know how upset you are about this and why you were too nervous to talk in Mr. Barnes's office."

"Thank you," Joshua said.

He wasn't sure what else to say.

"I'd like you to tell me now what happened inside you in your heart and head when you took my knife," his father said. "Tell me everything."

"Everything?"

"About the knife and why you needed it," his father said.

And this time Joshua did. He told his father how he had admired the knife for a long time, how he had imagined himself carrying it in the pocket of his jeans, how small he had felt after his first day in fourth grade and how the Swiss Army knife in his father's bureau drawer was just the solution.

When he finished, his father was staring over the steering wheel out the car window.

"So you see?" Joshua asked.

"Of course I see," his father said.

"I know what I did was terrible," Joshua said.

"Not terrible, Joshua," his father said. "Not after the year you've had. Not right but normal."

"Normal about the knife?" Joshua asked.

"No, not normal about the knife. That was very wrong, and I think you know that. Normal to want to feel important," his father said. "I understand that."

"So you're not mad?" Joshua said.

"No," his father said, pulling out of the parking lot

and turning left. "I'm upset and I certainly hope nothing like this will happen again, but I'm not mad."

"Do you know about Tommy Wilhelm and Billy Nickel?" Joshua asked when the car had stopped in front of the school.

"Your mother has told me about Tommy Wilhelm, and I believe Billy Nickel is the one who took the knife to the principal's office."

"Did Mom tell you that Tommy Wilhelm is like a dictator in charge of the fourth grade?" Joshua said. "That's why I feel the way I do."

"She has told me that. But Tommy Wilhelm doesn't have to be in charge, Joshua," his father said, kissing the top of Joshua's head. "Unless you let him. That's up to you."

"I guess you're right," Joshua said, climbing out of the front seat, closing the door of the Jeep, and waving good-bye to his father.

And suddenly lighthearted for the first time in days, he ran up the steps of Mirch Elementary two at a time.

Chapter Ten

After having lunch with his father, Joshua stopped to get his books for library and Spanish. Tommy Wilhelm and Billy Nickel were leaning against the lockers.

Joshua was thinking about what his father had said, about Tommy Wilhelm's power over every boy in the fourth grade, including him, maybe especially him, about Billy Nickel and why he'd turned in the knife to Mr. Barnes instead of giving it back to Joshua. He wished Andrew weren't sick. He needed someone to talk to about things. Maybe Amanda, since they'd gotten to be such good friends.

"So how's trouble, Joshua?" Tommy asked.

"What kind of trouble?" Joshua scrambled through his book bag for his Spanish book.

"Just sort of looks like you've been in trouble since you got promoted," Billy Nickel said.

"I guess I have," Joshua said.

"Too bad," Billy said.

"Yeah, very too bad," Joshua said. "I hate being in trouble."

And out of the blue, without even considering what he might say, without thinking, he turned to Billy Nickel.

"I guess I've been in a lot of trouble with your help." He put his Spanish book under his arm. "So I should say thanks a lot for turning me in to Mr. Barnes."

"Turning you in for what?" Billy Nickel asked, his blue eyes wide and innocent.

"The knife, lamebrain," Joshua said.

"I didn't turn *you* in," Billy Nickel said. "I turned the knife in. I didn't even know it was your knife."

"Right," Joshua said. "I showed it to you on the playground at recess. You knew exactly whose knife it was, and that's why you turned it in."

"Oh, yeah," Billy said. "I sort of remember now."

A crowd was beginning to gather around the lockers. Ethan had wandered up with Douglas and Rusty. Brendan came in from the playground and hung up his coat.

"Now I remember, too," Tommy Wilhelm said. "It was the knife you got for your birthday."

"Wrong," Joshua said.

"Well, that's what you said." Tommy shrugged.

"But it's not exactly true," Joshua said. "The knife doesn't belong to me."

And he could hardly believe what he was saying into the air so everyone around could hear and know him as a liar and a thief. But he couldn't help himself. The words were flying out of his mouth like kites.

"It's the knife that I stole from my father to impress you guys so you'd be nice to me," he said.

"What guys?" Tommy Wilhelm asked.

"What are you talking about?" Billy Nickel asked.

"Who do you need to impress?" Tommy asked.

Joshua's heart was beating too hard and his knees were noodles, but somehow he felt sort of wonderful, as if he were on the soccer field and had the ball and a clear field in front of him, a real chance of scoring, just the goalie in the distance standing in the middle of the goal.

"I guess he's talking about you guys," Ethan said quietly.

"Us?" Tommy asked, a little smirk curling around his lips.

"What about us?" Billy Nickel asked.

"Everybody's afraid of you," Joshua said. "Right?" He looked at Rusty, who looked down at the ground. He looked at Brendan.

"What's to be afraid of?" Tommy asked, his face going red as cherries.

"Yeah?" Billy Nickel added. "What?"

"Nothing," Joshua said, taking a deep breath so he wouldn't faint dead away on the floor, so he would be able to walk down the hall to the fourth-grade classroom without dying of a heart attack. "There's nothing to be afraid of at all."

And as he walked past Mrs. Goodwin's third grade, waving to her, he could feel the eyes of the fourth-grade boys burning on his back.

"Wow," Rusty said, passing Joshua seated at his desk with his Spanish book open. "That was something."

Joshua shrugged.

Ethan passed him a note just before the bell. "Not bad, Bates. Did you really steal the knife?"

Joshua nodded.

Señora Supervia asked for quiet, but Douglas, leaning over his desk, asked Joshua if he wanted to come over after school.

"I can't today," Joshua said.

"Maybe you can spend the night on Friday," Douglas said.

Señora Supervia told Douglas to sit in the front of the room and told Joshua to be quiet or he'd be sent to Mr. Barnes's office.

*   *   *

After Spanish, Billy Nickel ran after Joshua, who was walking with Douglas and Ethan on their way to the library.

"Wait up, you guys," Billy said, rushing to catch up with them.

They stopped and waited.

"Listen, Joshua," Billy said, out of breath. "I didn't mean to do that. I forgot it was your knife."

"S'okay," Joshua said.

"You didn't get in a lot of trouble, did you?" he asked.

"I didn't get expelled, if that's what you're asking," Joshua said, walking into the library.

Tommy Wilhelm was already in the library, sitting at a long table, his book opened, pretending to read. Joshua sat down across from him.

"Hi," Tommy said.

"Hi," Joshua replied. He heard Billy Nickel ask the librarian if he could be excused to go to the nurse because he thought he was going to throw up.

"He's not really sick, you know," Tommy said. "He's kind of a chicken."

"I thought he was your best friend," Joshua said.

Tommy shrugged. "Not really. Not any longer."

Joshua opened his library book, rested his chin in his hands, and tried to read, but he couldn't concentrate.

Soon, he thought, checking the clock over the librarian's desk, this day, Wednesday, his third day in the fourth grade, would be over and he could go home and tell Amanda everything that had happened with Tommy Wilhelm and Billy Nickel and all of his new friends in the fourth grade.

They would sit on his bed with Plutarch licking his yellow belly and listen to the sounds of their mother cooking dinner in the kitchen, of Georgianna, already put to bed for the night, squealing in her crib, of their father's car pulling into the driveway.

"You're amazing, Joshua," he imagined Amanda saying to him. "I can't believe you're my very own brother."

"Well, I am," Joshua would say. "Your amazing brother, Joshua T. Bates."

And then their mother would call them to dinner and they'd fly down the stairs, through the front hall, into the kitchen, and fall into their chairs.

"I guess you want to hear about how fourth grade was today," Joshua would say to his mother and father.

"Of course," they'd reply. "We want to know everything."

"Well," Joshua would begin. "I think I'm going to like it a lot."

Susan Shreve is the author of many books for children, including *The Flunking of Joshua T. Bates; Joshua T. Bates Takes Charge; The Goalie; Lucy Forever and Miss Rosetree, Shrinks* (winner of the Edgar Allan Poe Award); and *The Gift of the Girl Who Couldn't Hear.*

A graduate of the University of Pennsylvania, Ms. Shreve is a creative writing professor at George Mason University. She lives in Washington, D.C.

The Flunking of Joshua T. Bates

by Susan Shreve

It's the worst possible end to a great summer vacation: Joshua Bates finds out he has to repeat the third grade. His teachers say he needs another year "to mature." What do they expect from a nine-year-old? A beard?

The first day of school is a complete nightmare. The fourth graders think he's a freak, the kids in his new class are babies, and his teacher looks like a two-ton tank. Joshua is totally miserable. Will he ever catch up — or is he stuck in the third grade forever?

"Touching, funny, and realistic."
—*School Library Journal*

"Crisply humorous."
—*The Bulletin of the Center for Children's Books*

Joshua T. Bates Takes Charge

by Susan Shreve

Joshua T. Bates is no stranger to bullies. After he flunked the third grade, Joshua became big Tommy Wilhelm's prime target. But it's fifth grade now, and Tommy and his gang, the Nerds Out, have a new victim: Sean O'Malley, the dorky kid with the Mickey Mouse lunchbox. He's little, he's wimpy, and—to Joshua's relief—he's taking up all of the gang's time.

The trouble is, Sean thinks Joshua is his new best friend. Now Joshua has a tough decision to make. Should he stick up for the geek—and risk his own neck?

"Welcome back, Joshua T. Bates!"
—*School Library Journal*

"A perceptive story that makes it plain what it's like to be an outcast and also what it takes to be a hero."
—*Booklist*